Friendly, Scared, and Working Dogs

Written by
Linda Johansen

Art by Kim Sponaugle

The Adventures of Miss Aspen Lu

Friendly, Scared, and Working Dogs
The Adventures of Miss Aspen Lu
Written by Linda Johansen
Illustrated by Kim Sponaugle

FIRST EDITION

ISBN: Hardback   978-1-0880-4019-5

ASPEN LEAF Publishing

Dedicated to:
Aspen Lu, whose life goal is to cuddle all the puppies,
and Scout, whose life goal is to receive all the cuddles.

Aspen Lu loves puppy dogs, and always wants to play.
She would stay outside and pet them, every single day.

When she sees a doggy, while out walking in the park,
She always wants to hug them, even if they bark.

She knows to ask permission from her mommy first of all,
But should also ask the owner, or the one who throws the ball.

Sometimes they'll say,
"Yes, that's fine," and
all of you can play!

Can I pet your puppies?

Of course, thanks for asking.

But other times the dog is

grumpy,

scared,

or busy training on that day.

Some puppies are happy, friendly,
and cute-just like you.

But sometimes they're **nervous**, **scared**, **angry** or **blue**.

Sometimes all of us
get scared, and frightened

of new things.
So, let's take it slow,

be nice to them
and see just
what this brings

There is another type of dog to note, whose numbers are quite few.

No honey. That is a special kind of dog...that is a working dog.

Can I pet the dog in the vest?

Some are service dogs for people who are blind and cannot see.

And Medical Dogs help others, so that they can live like you and me.

Some dogs help cops and soldiers, to catch all the bad guys.

"WOW that's neat," said Aspen Lu.
"Can they even fly through the skies?"

These dogs are busy working,
they have a job to do.

But why can't
we pet them?

We just can't distract them, my little Aspen Lu.

But don't you worry, they run around without their vests,
for a little bit each day.

There are many different types of dogs it's true.

And if we treat them just right... they can be here to Love me and You.

CPSIA information can be obtained
at www.ICGtesting.com
Printed in the USA
LVHW070633151222
735218LV00009B/276